The
Persuading Stick

The
Persuading Stick

JOHN ROWE TOWNSEND

Lothrop, Lee & Shepard Books
New York

First U.S. Edition 1 2 3 4 5 6 7 8 9 10

Library of Congress Cataloging in Publication Data
Townsend, John Rowe.   The persuading stick.
Summary: A quiet English girl becomes more assertive with the help of a magic stick. [1. Magic—Fiction. 2. Assertiveness (Psychology)—Fiction. 3. England—Fiction] I. Title. PZ7.T6637Pe 1987   [Fic]   86-27720
ISBN 0-688-07260-7

The Persuading Stick

1 ———————————————————

When Beth and Sarah were out of school first, they waited for Katherine before they set off home.

When Katherine and Sarah were out of school first, they waited for Beth.

But when Beth and Katherine were out first, they set off at once and never waited for Sarah. They didn't even think of Sarah. They just talked away to each other fifteen to the dozen, all the way along Barrow Lane to the new houses at Spinney Close. That was where Beth and Katherine and Sarah all lived.

Beth was dark and sturdy and had bold brown

eyes. Katherine was thin and pretty and very fair, with blue-gray eyes. Sarah was just ordinary. She had plain, straight, mousy-colored hair, and nobody could tell her what color her eyes were. "Hazel," said Sarah's mum when asked about it. "Much more interesting than blue or brown." But Sarah thought they were just mixed.

Beth was good at games, and when there were teams she was always chosen first. Katherine had been Queen of the May, and was Mary in the school nativity play. Sarah was one of the last to be picked at games, and in the nativity play she was a back-row angel.

And in her own house Sarah was the youngest. There were Donald and Robin ahead of her. Donald was nearly grown up and had left school. Robin was a year older than Sarah, and he would sometimes play with her if his own friends were not playing. But if he did, he had to be boss.

Mum said that the first words Sarah ever spoke were, "Me too." Sarah didn't remember that. But one day when Beth and Katherine wouldn't let Sarah play and were teasing her, they mimicked her voice calling, "Wait for me! Wait for me!" After that Sarah tried not to call. It didn't make any difference. They never waited for her anyway. Not until the day came when she couldn't bear being left behind anymore. And that was the day she found the persuading stick.

It was on a Friday in April, soon after term had started. Beth and Katherine were ahead of Sarah, walking home from school along Barrow Lane. Sarah walked fast, trying to catch up with them. They knew she was there, although they pretended not to. When Sarah walked faster, they walked faster too.

At the bend in Barrow Lane, instead of going on toward Spinney Close, they turned off the other way, along a path to the canal bank. Sarah went that way too, behind them. Then they took notice of her. Both of them turned round and waited. Sarah came up to them.

"Go back!" said Beth.

"Why?" asked Sarah.

"Because you're not supposed to come down here. You're supposed to go straight home."

"So are you!" said Sarah.

"We're not. We're older than you."

"You're only a little bit older."

"I'm half a year older," said Beth.

"Katherine isn't. Her birthday's only a week before mine."

"Well, you're not coming *anyway*!" said Beth.

"I'll tell. I'll tell that you've gone to the canal bank." All the Spinney Close children were forbidden to go down to the canal.

"Tell if you like," said Katherine. "Tattletale . . ."

But they knew Sarah wouldn't tell. Sarah never did tell. She often said she would, but she never actually did.

Beth and Katherine turned their backs on Sarah and walked away from her with their heads in the air. That was the moment when it came over her that she wasn't going to put up with this. She would *make* them let her go along with them. She didn't know how she'd do it, but she knew she would. She followed them, fuming, down to the towpath.

In summer the towpath was an interesting place to walk because so many boats came past. There were great long chugging narrowboats, steered from behind by a person holding a tiller. There were smart, zippy, expensive-looking cruisers, and there were little plastic boats with engines that went put-put-put. There were even boats with people rowing. But April was early in the season, and most boats were still tied up. Nothing came along. Not that Sarah had eyes for her surroundings anyway. She was much too angry.

A little way along the towpath was a big, tall clump of withered reeds and stalks of old plants, with new growth just coming through. Beth and Katherine walked straight past the clump, side by side. They kept looking round and giggling. They were enjoying not letting Sarah join them. And the more they looked round and giggled, the crosser Sarah got.

4

But as she passed the clump, something took her mind off her anger. It was a powerful sense of excitement, as if something remarkable was going to happen. The excitement was radiating from that clump and drawing her toward it.

Along with the urge to go to the clump came other strange sensations. There was a faint scent of something fragrant—but the scent wasn't in her nose, it was in her head. Or it was as if there were nice sounds, but sounds that didn't come to her ears, only to her imagination. Or as if there was something special to look at, but just out of sight, though she knew it was there. Whatever it was, it was telling her that it was hidden, waiting for her to find it.

When she was past the clump she felt the call, stronger than ever, coming to her from behind. She turned and walked slowly back. And as soon as she peered into the clump she knew what was calling to her. It drew her eyes and her hands, both together, so that she found herself reaching out for it. It was a stick, about eight inches long, with a rough, silvery surface. It was in among some hollow stalks, and at first sight it looked like a short, frosted stem of cow parsley.

When she picked it from the clump, it came out without any effort on her part, and settled into her hand. It was pleasantly warm to hold and slightly springy, with a feel to it as if it were a living creature. As she held it, the scent-that-wasn't and the sound-that-wasn't died away, and in their place a sense of power and confidence flowed into her.

Beth and Katherine, farther along the towpath, had noticed that Sarah had stopped. They stopped too, watching from a distance as Sarah reached into the clump. She held up the stick and called to them, "Beth! Katherine! Come here!" She willed them to come, with the strength the stick gave her.

For a moment Beth and Katherine stood still. Then, slowly and as if reluctantly, they came back along the towpath. They walked together, side by side, in step.

Beth said, "What happened? What did you do?" Then, looking at the stick, "What's that?"

"Something I found."

"Let's have a look."

Sarah held out the stick, but kept a firm hold on it.

"It's just an old stick," said Beth.

"It's not just an old stick. It's special."

"What's special about it?"

Sarah didn't know what made her answer as she did. It was as if she heard the answer coming out of her mouth without knowing what it was going to be.

"It's a persuading stick," she said.

"What's a persuading stick?"

"It makes people do what I want them to do."

Katherine looked at the stick round-eyed. "Like a magic wand?" she asked.

"Sort of like a magic wand. But it doesn't do any other kind of magic." Sarah didn't know how she knew that, but she did.

"Go on!" said Beth. "You're daft. Bananas. Bonkers. Off your trolley. It's just a stick. We saw you pull it out from among all those old reeds and stuff."

"It's a persuading stick," said Sarah firmly. "It persuaded *you*, didn't it? I made you come back along the towpath just now. You *had* to come back."

Beth and Katherine looked at each other. Katherine said, "I did feel as if something was pulling us back."

For a moment Beth looked uneasy. Then she said, "It didn't do anything to me. I just decided to come back, that's all. You didn't make me, nor did your silly old stick. A stick couldn't make anybody do anything."

"This one can," said Sarah.

"Prove it, then. Make me do something."

"All right," said Sarah. She felt absolutely confident. She knew the stick would make Beth do as she was told. "Bend down and touch your toes."

Beth looked steadily at Sarah. She opened her mouth and started to say "No." Sarah looked steadily back at her. Beth closed her mouth. Then, very slowly, she bent forward and touched her toes. She straightened up.

"I only did it because I wanted to," she said. Then, as if not sure, "Didn't I?"

"I think it was the stick," said Katherine. "Or else it was the funny way Sarah looked at you."

"It was the stick," said Sarah.

"It wasn't."

"I'll prove it. Jump up and down."

"No," said Beth.

"Go on, jump up and down!"

"I won't!" said Beth. She glowered. Then, in spite of what she'd just said, she began jumping up and down.

"Higher than that!" said Sarah.

Beth jumped higher. She jumped and jumped. After a while she said, still jumping, "I'm tired."

"Keep on jumping!" said Sarah.

"I can't! I haven't any breath left!"

Sarah said, "Go on. Jump some more!"

Beth jumped two or three more times. She was looking distressed. Katherine said, "Let her stop, Sarah!"

Sarah relented. "All right," she said, "you can stop now."

Beth stopped. She was panting. Katherine said, "Tell *me* something, Sarah!"

While Beth got her breath back, Sarah told Katherine again and again to bend and stretch her arms, then to twirl around. Katherine obeyed her every time.

Beth watched, frowning. After a while she said, "Let me have a go with the stick!"

Sarah said, "No."

"Oh, come on! Just a lend! I'll give you it back!"

Sarah said, "No, it's mine!"

"It's not yours. You just picked it up. It isn't yours any more than anybody else's."

"It *is* mine. It came into my hand. It was there for *me*."

"Give it to me. Or I'll take it!"

"It won't let you," said Sarah. "It—it'll sting you!"

Beth reached out to grab it. But when Beth's hand was nearly on the stick Sarah yelped loudly, she didn't know why. Beth yelped in turn and pulled her hand back.

"*Did* it sting, Beth?" asked Katherine anxiously.

Beth looked a bit shaky.

"I *think* it did," she said. "It was like—it was like an electric shock."

"That was its sting!" said Sarah. "I warned you, didn't I?"

"I don't like it," said Katherine. She sounded frightened.

"If you don't touch it," said Sarah, "it won't hurt you. And it's time to go home. Our mums will wonder where we are." She held up the stick. "Come on. We're all going home."

Beth and Katherine didn't argue. They all set off back along the towpath, then up the path that led to Barrow Lane. Sarah went first. She didn't look round to see if the other two were behind her. She knew they'd follow.

When they got to Spinney Close, Katherine asked, "Would the stick work on grown-ups, Sarah?"

"I don't know," said Sarah. "It might."

"Try it!" said Beth. "Try it on your mum!"

"What shall I ask her to do?"

"Ask for *us* to come to tea!" said Beth promptly.

Sarah said, "I don't think she likes people coming to tea all of a sudden. My brother Donald brought his girlfriend to tea last week without telling Mum beforehand. She didn't say anything, but she was cross afterward. Though p'raps it was because she doesn't *like* his girlfriend much."

"Well," said Beth, "if the stick works, it'll make her have us whether she wants to or not."

Sarah said uneasily, "I don't want to make my mum do something she doesn't like doing."

"If you want us to believe in the stick," said Beth, "you'll do it."

Beth was more like herself now. She went on, "I mean, when I touched my toes and jumped up and down, it was only a kind of game. And the stick didn't really give me a shock. I thought it did, just for a moment, because of the way you yelped."

It looked as if Beth had almost stopped believing. Sarah didn't want that.

"All right," she said, "I'll make my mum ask you to tea."

"And make her give us beans on toast," said Beth.

"She doesn't like baked beans," said Sarah. "There mightn't be any in the house."

"If your stick works, there'll be beans," said Beth.

"It doesn't magic things out of nothing," Sarah told her. "It only persuades. It couldn't persuade a person to give you beans if they didn't *have* any beans, could it?"

Beth and Katherine considered the matter.

Beth said, "A real magic wand could magic a can of beans out of nothing. Or a hundred cans of beans, if you asked it."

"Or a thousand cans of beans!" said Katherine, and giggled.

"Or a million cans of beans!" said Beth.

"We don't want a million cans of beans!" said Sarah crossly. "Anyway, I keep telling you, it isn't a magic wand, it's a persuading stick."

Beth and Katherine went to tell their mums they were back from school. Sarah pushed the persuading stick as far as it would go into her jeans pocket, and held the end of it in her hand. It looked quite natural, and nobody would notice.

As she approached her own gate, her brother

Donald came out. His shoulders were hunched and his eyes on the ground. He didn't even see Sarah until she called, "Donald!" Then he looked up and gave her a rather weary grin.

"Hello, Tiddles!" he said.

"Don't call me Tiddles!"

Donald ruffled her hair. "Okay," he said, *"Sarah!"* and grinned again. Then he moved on. Donald was fond of Sarah, but he didn't have much time to talk to her these days. He always had other things on his mind. Or other people. Or one other person, anyway. That was Gemma James. Donald had been going out with Gemma for a month, and spent all the time he could with her. He was probably on his way now to Churchill Towers, the high block of flats where Gemma lived.

Sarah opened the back door of the house. There was a smell of cigarette smoke in the kitchen. That was because Donald had been there. Nobody else in the family smoked. And Mum was in the kitchen, looking worried. She often looked worried when she'd been talking to Donald.

"Hello, dear," she said, and kissed Sarah, but her thoughts seemed far away.

"Mum, will you . . . ?" Sarah began, still holding the stick in her pocket.

"Yes, dear?"

"Mum, will you . . . ? Mum, I want . . ."

Then there was a knock on the door. Beth and

Katherine had arrived, a little breathless from running.

"Hello, there!" Mum said, coming back to earth. "Come in, both of you!"

Sarah clutched the stick more tightly and said, "I want them to come to tea!"

"Well," said Mum. "Yes, they can come. But it's short notice, isn't it? It's nearly teatime now. And I haven't got anything special in the house." She turned to Beth and Katherine. "Do your mothers know you're here?"

"Oh, yes!" Beth told her.

"Please, Mum," said Sarah, "I want you to give them beans. On toast."

"I didn't know you liked beans, Sarah."

"I want you to give us beans today," said Sarah. She squeezed on the stick. It was comfortably warm in her hand. She was sure it was going to work.

"I expect that could be managed," said Mum, smiling.

Beth and Katherine looked at each other, impressed.

"You see? It *does* work!" Sarah whispered.

"What was that, dear?" asked Mum.

"Nothing," said Sarah. Suddenly she was feeling tired, as if she'd used up a lot of energy.

2 _____

Ker-PAT! Ker-PAT! Ker-PAT!

That was the sound that woke Sarah up next morning. She heard it first through a dream, and then, slowly, she woke up and knew it was actually happening. And she knew what it was. It was Robin, the younger of her two brothers, bouncing his ball against the wall of the house, below her window.

Sarah got out of bed, ran to the window, and leaned out. "Yoo-hoo!" she called.

But Robin didn't take any notice. He was counting. Sarah could just hear his muttered words.

"Forty-one, forty-two, forty-three . . ." Each time the ball hit the wall, Robin waited for it to bounce on the ground, then hit it with his hand against the wall again. He was practicing tennis. Robin didn't have a tennis racket, but he was hoping to get one for his birthday. In the meantime, he played against the wall with the flat of his hand. He counted the number of times he got the ball back. Once he had scored two hundred.

Sarah ran downstairs. It wasn't breakfast time yet. Breakfast was late on Saturdays. But it was a fine spring morning, and Robin was up and about. She went outside and stood near him.

"Go away!" said Robin. "Sixty-eight, sixty-nine, seventy . . ."

"Let me have a turn!" said Sarah.

"No. Seventy-four, seventy-five, seventy-six . . . Now look what you've made me do!"

Robin had hit the ball on the slant, and it shot off the wall at an angle, so that he missed it.

"Let me have a turn *now*!" said Sarah.

"I told you, no! One, two, three. And get out of the way. Seven, eight, nine. Go on! I don't want you! Ten . . ."

Robin never bothered to be polite to Sarah.

She started slowly back into the house. Then she remembered the persuading stick. She'd put it in her top drawer the night before. It hadn't been mentioned while Beth and Katherine were at the house. Sarah had felt tired all evening, and by bedtime she'd almost stopped believing in the stick. After all, it hadn't performed any miracles. Beth and Katherine had behaved as they might have behaved anyway, and Mum would have let them come to tea and given them baked beans if she'd been asked in the ordinary way. Maybe the persuading stick was just a funny bit of stick she'd found on the canal bank.

But it was worth a try.

She went to her room and opened the drawer. And at once the stick spoke to her as it had done on the canal bank. Not with a voice. It spoke with that silent sound that went straight into her head without going through her ears. It was a kind of unheard music. And once again there was a very slight fragrance, rather like that of the potpourri in Mum's room.

She picked up the stick, and it settled into her hand as if being picked up was just what it wanted. It was slightly warm and slightly rough and slightly springy and altogether pleasant to hold.

She went into the garden again, but this time she didn't go near Robin, because she wanted to walk around by herself for a bit, just enjoying the silvery springiness of the stick.

It was a glorious day, with a slight breeze that carried on it all the scents of all the back gardens. Nobody was around except herself and Robin and the next-door neighbors' cat, which sat quietly on a shed roof, washing itself. Sarah was full of happiness. The stick made her feel that she could do anything she liked, and everything was all right. Everything was always going to be all right.

She arrived back at where Robin was still patting his ball against the wall. He was intent on what he was doing. "Hundred-and-two, hundred-and-three, hundred-and-four," Robin chanted. Sarah stood watching him for a minute. She wanted to try the stick again. As before, she held it in her jeans pocket, with her hand on the end that stuck out.

"Miss it!" she whispered in Robin's direction. "Miss the ball!"

As she whispered, her fingers closed more tightly on the persuading stick, and she thought it felt slightly warmer. The ball flew off the wall, rather high, and Robin had to run back to reach it. He'd done that often before. But this time, as he turned and raised his hand to hit the ball, he hesitated. The ball went past his hand, bounced a second time, rolled across the grass, and came to rest against the garden fence.

Robin was looking at his hand in a puzzled way. He turned and saw Sarah.

"That was *your* fault!" he said, picking up the ball. But Sarah could tell from the way he spoke that he was still puzzled. He didn't really think she had anything to do with it. He was blaming her because she was his sister and he always blamed her for things.

"*Now* let me have a turn!" said Sarah, still clutching the stick.

"No!" said Robin. But as he said it his hand opened. The ball lay on his palm. He looked at it. His fingers half closed on it. Then they opened again.

"Oh, all *right!*" he said crossly. He threw the ball toward her, turned his back, and stomped away as if to go into the house.

"Come back, Robin," Sarah called.

Robin turned. Very slowly and reluctantly he came toward her.

"We'll play together. I'll play against you," Sarah said.

"I don't want . . ." he began. Then he paused. After a few seconds he said, "Oh, all right. If you *must.*" He went on, "I can't understand you, Sarah Casson. You don't usually *want* to play. Why are you so eager *now?*"

But it seemed to Sarah that he was only grumbling. He would play with her.

The stick wouldn't be safe in her pocket while she played. Sarah didn't want Robin to see it. She went to pick up the ball, and while she was doing so she put down the stick in a flower bed. They started to play, alternately hitting the ball against the wall. It was a game that Robin always won. Soon he was winning now.

"Miss it!" Sarah whispered under her breath two or three times. But Robin didn't miss it. It looked as though the persuading stick would only work if she was actually holding it.

They played together for five minutes. Robin's temper improved. He liked winning. Then Sarah took a desperate swipe at the ball. It hit the wall hard, bounced from it on a high upward curve, and flew through the air toward the fence. No, not *toward* the fence. *Over* the fence, and into Mrs. Sellars's garden.

Robin said a rude word. "*Now* you've done it!" he went on. "She'll be watching, the old cow!"

Mrs. Sellars's kitchen looked straight onto her garden. She hated it when a ball came over the fence. She hated it even more when a child came over the fence looking for the ball. If the child was small enough, she would dash out, capture it, and march it back to its parents to make a complaint. This had happened to Sarah once and to Robin three times. And last time it had happened, their mother had told them there would be lots of trouble if it happened again.

Robin and Sarah looked at each other in dismay. Robin was dismayed because it was his ball. Sarah was dismayed because she was the one who'd sent it over the fence. If they didn't get it back themselves, they would never see it again. Other neighbors would throw a ball back or give its owner permission to go and look for it. Not Mrs. Sellars.

Sarah could feel Robin's fury building up.

"*You* can go for it!" he said. "Or else buy me another!"

Until that morning, Sarah would never have dared to tackle Mrs. Sellars. Even the thought of it made her feel scared inside. Then she remembered the persuading stick.

"All right," she said. "I'll go and ask Mrs. Sellars if I can get it."

Robin was surprised. "You wouldn't dare!" he said.

"I would. I *will*."

"She won't give it to you," Robin said. "You *know* she won't. She never does."

"I bet she will!" said Sarah.

"All right, then, go!" said Robin. "But I'm not coming. It wasn't me that sent it over."

Sarah still didn't want Robin to see the persuading stick. If he saw it, he'd ask her what it was, and if she told him, he'd jeer at her. That would be no help at all. But at the moment the stick was in the flower bed where she'd put it, and there was no way she could pick it up without being seen.

"Well, go on, then," said Robin. "What are you waiting for? Nobody's stopping you."

"I'll go when you've gone indoors," said Sarah.

"Oh, yes?" said Robin. He was disbelieving her again. "You get that ball back," he said, "or you can buy me a new one!"

At that moment, Mum opened the kitchen window. "Come along!" she said. "Breakfast time!"

Robin went into the house at once. He liked his meals. As soon as he was out of the way, Sarah picked up the persuading stick and ran out through the garden gate. Mrs. Sellars's garden backed onto their own, but to get to her front door you had to go to the top of Spinney Close and back down Hillside Avenue.

Sarah was out of breath when she reached Mrs. Sellars's house. She had a moment of panic. Then her hand closed on the stick and felt its slight, reassuring warmth. She walked boldly up the garden path and rang Mrs. Sellars's bell.

Mrs. Sellars came to the door at once. She was tall and thin and sour-faced. She lived with her only child, Jason, who was in Sarah's class at school. There wasn't a Mr. Sellars. Neighbors said he'd escaped from Mrs. Sellars years ago.

She opened the door an inch or two.

"Well?" she said.

"Can I get my ball from your garden?" Sarah asked.

"No, you can not!"

Mrs. Sellars was about to slam the door. There

was only a split second in which to act. Sarah squeezed the stick nervously.

"Please let me!" she said.

The door, which had been closing, stayed ajar. Mrs. Sellars and Sarah looked at each other. There was the puzzled expression on Mrs. Sellars's face that Sarah had already seen on Beth's and Katherine's and Robin's. Then she spoke in a slow and grating voice, as if the words were being dragged out of her.

"All right," she said. "Go and get it. Be quick."

Sarah ran to the far end of the garden. Luckily the ball was lying on the grass, easy to see. Sarah picked it up and returned round the side of the house. Mrs. Sellars had come outside and was watching her with a mixture of crossness and bewilderment. Her face was as sour as ever.

Sarah stopped, and a wild impulse came upon her.

"Why don't you smile, Mrs. Sellars?" she asked. "*Please* smile!" Her fingers tightened once more on the stick.

A gruesome death's-head smile came over Mrs. Sellars's face. She didn't look amused at all. She looked as if the smile was positively painful to her. It seemed to Sarah that although the persuading stick might make people do things, it didn't have the power to make them *like* doing whatever it was. She gasped out a "Thank you" and fled.

3

"So the dreadful monster let you get your ball!"
said Dad, grinning.

Sarah had joined the rest of the family at the
breakfast table. All except Donald. Donald was still
in bed. Donald stayed in bed most mornings.

"From what Robin said, I thought we'd never
see you again," Dad went on. "I thought she'd
swallow you alive."

"You don't know Mrs. Sellars!" said Mum to Dad.
"I'm glad we don't have to deal with her this
morning."

"I don't suppose she's so bad really," said Dad.

"Oh, she *is*!" said Robin. He was looking at Sarah with new respect. Sarah had done what he didn't dare to do, and she'd come back triumphant.

"Well, if Mrs. Sellars is as bad as all that," said Dad, "the conclusion must be that Sarah is extremely persuasive."

Sarah didn't say anything about the stick. She was feeling tired again, although earlier on she'd been full of energy.

Dad drank up his coffee and asked, "Well, what do people want to do today?"

Mum said, "As little as possible, I should think. It's a lovely day for April. Nice enough for sitting in the garden."

Dad said, "Or working in it. That's what I should be doing, I suppose. But I don't feel like it this morning. Let's all go out somewhere."

"To the fish farm!" said Robin.

Dad said, "Oh, *no*! Not the fish farm again!"

Robin and Sarah liked going to the fish farm. There were huge tanks the size of swimming pools, full of trout. You could buy bags of fish food to throw to the trout, and they would lift their heads out of the water to take it. And the farm also sold tropical fish, brilliant little fishes in blue and gold and silver. Robin loved tropical fish and always wanted to buy some. Mum and Dad never did. They'd had lots of tropical fish and all of the fish had died. But Robin always thought the next one would survive.

Dad said, "I am not, absolutely *not*, going to the fish farm today. Nothing would persuade me."

"Not even your persuasive daughter?" asked Mum.

"Not even my persuasive daughter."

"I should have thought," said Mum to Dad with a mischievous look in her eye, "that in comparison with Mrs. Sellars, you would be a pushover."

"Well, what about it?" said Robin to Sarah. "You got the ball back. Get Dad to take us to the fish farm!"

Sarah fingered the persuading stick in her jeans pocket. It didn't quite have that feeling of being alive that it had had before breakfast. She squeezed hard on it.

"I'm telling you," Dad was saying, "there's nothing doing, whatever anyone says. Let me spell it out once and for all, and then we'll drop the subject. I will not go to the fish farm today." His voice slowed down as he spoke. "Er . . ." He hesitated. "Well, I . . . I don't *think* we'll go to the fish farm." His eyes were on Sarah's face. For a moment he was silent. Then he said, "Of course, if we *did* go to the fish farm, we could buy some trout for when your aunt Jenny and uncle Keith come to tea tomorrow. So it might be quite a good idea after all."

He added, to Mum, "Don't you think so, Helen?"

Mum and Robin were staring at Dad. There was a puzzled look on his face—the same puzzled look that Sarah had seen on the faces of Beth, Katherine, Robin, and Mrs. Sellars when they did what she wanted.

"Did I say we'd go to the fish farm?" Dad said. "I did? Well, then, we'd better go to the fish farm. Finish up your breakfast, folks. We'll go as soon as you're ready."

"You did it again, Sis!" said Robin admiringly. But Sarah wasn't listening. She felt deeply weary. She went to her room and took the stick from her pocket. It felt cold and lifeless. She put it in her top drawer and lay down on her bed. Five minutes later Mum came to her.

"Are you all right, darling?" Mum asked.

"Yes," said Sarah. "Just a bit tired."

"At this time of day? That's not like you. And you're looking a bit pale, Sarah. Are you *sure* you're all right?"

Sarah nodded. She didn't feel ill. Just tired.

"Well, you can lie down a bit longer if you like," said Mum. "Dad and I have just decided we won't go to the fish farm till after lunch. There are things he wants to do in the garden first . . . Are you listening, Sarah?"

But Sarah was asleep. She slept for an hour. Then

she got up and went downstairs. Mum was in the kitchen.

"How are you now?" Mum inquired.

"Fine."

"You look much better. You've got your color back."

Sarah helped Dad in the garden for a while. She was very thoughtful. After lunch, when she went to get ready for the trip to the fish farm, she left her drawer closed, with the persuading stick inside. She didn't want to do any more persuading today.

Mum drove the car. They went out of Spinney Close and uphill through the new development. Half a mile along on their right was the high concrete-and-glass apartment block, Churchill Towers, where Donald's girlfriend Gemma lived. Opposite Churchill Towers, and as different from it as you could possibly get, was a little stone house-and-shop, a hundred years old at least, which had been engulfed by all the new buildings. This was old Mrs. Goodier's sweet shop. Mum stopped the car in front of it.

"I'll buy a box of after-dinner mints for when Keith and Jenny come," she said. "We don't really need them, but I like to give Mrs. Goodier a bit of business. She needs it, poor old soul."

"Buy us an ice cream, Mum!" urged Robin.

"Now, now, Robin," said Mum. "There's a limit to what I can do for the sake of Mrs. Goodier. And what cheek, asking for ice cream when you've only just had your lunch! You don't want ice cream now!"

"I do!" said Robin.

"I guess kids always want ice cream," said Dad.

"Well, you're not having one!" said Mum firmly.

Robin nudged Sarah. *"You* ask her!" he whispered.

"I heard that!" said Dad. "Well, maybe Mrs. Sellars and I couldn't resist Sarah, but I bet her mother can. Eh, Mum?"

"I certainly can!" said Mum. She turned to look at Sarah. "Try me and see!"

Sarah hadn't said anything. She didn't say anything now. She didn't want to persuade Mum. She didn't want an ice cream anyway. She was glad she didn't have the persuading stick with her. She didn't want to do anything that wasn't ordinary. She looked back at Mum with troubled eyes.

After a few seconds, Mum burst out laughing. "Well!" she said to Dad. "I begin to understand. When Sarah looks at you like that, you just can't say no, can you?" And to Robin and Sarah she said, "All right, kids, you can have your ice cream, and if you're sick it's your own fault!"

Robin was delighted. "Give me the money, then!" he said. "I'll get the mints for you as well."

Sarah felt tears welling up in her eyes. "I d-don't want any ice cream," she said. "I didn't want to persuade you. I wasn't even *trying*. You don't *understand*!"

"I certainly don't!" said Mum as she gave Robin the money. "What an odd child you are, Sarah! Sometimes I don't know what to make of you!"

Sarah gulped back sobs. Robin dashed into the shop and came back a minute later with a box of mints and his ice cream.

"These ice cream bars are good!" he said. "Fancy not wanting one!" And then, generously, to Sarah, "Have a lick of mine!" But Sarah turned her face away.

4

For everyone except Sarah, the trip to the trout farm was a success. Mum and Dad were pleased because they bought half a dozen gleaming rainbow trout for Sunday tea. Robin was pleased because he managed, without any help from Sarah, to persuade Dad to buy him a vivid little fish called a Cambridge Blue. He carried it home in a plastic bag, for transfer to the glass bowl left empty by the death of the previous inhabitant.

Sarah had a sad afternoon. She'd always enjoyed going to the fish farm before, but something had changed inside her since last time. She hated to see the bright bodies of the trout wrapped up for Dad to take away, and to think of the eager thousands of them thronging the huge tanks and facing the same fate. She even felt sorry for Robin's little blue fish, which she was sure would be bored and lonely in the round glass bowl.

"Leave her alone," said Mum to Dad when he tried to cheer her up with a joke and a bit of teasing. "She'll come round in her own good time."

In the evening, Sarah watched TV with the family. She stayed away from her own room. She was a little afraid of the persuading stick, sitting there in her drawer. In spite of her fear, she felt an impulse from time to time to go and get it out, and feel its pleasant cool roughness in her hand. And she was afraid of her own impulse. There was something dangerous about the stick. In the end, she was reluctant to go to bed.

Mum and Dad were surprised. Sarah was good about going to bed as a rule. It was Robin who always tried to stay up past his bedtime.

"You're sure she isn't sickening for something?" asked Dad.

"If she was sickening for something, she'd *want* to go to bed," said Mum crisply.

At last, three-quarters asleep, Sarah made her way upstairs. She undressed quickly, aware all the time of the persuading stick in its drawer and keeping well away from it. And once she'd jumped into bed she felt safe, just as she'd done when she was smaller and afraid of shadows on the stairs. By the time Mum came up to kiss her good night, she was fast asleep.

When she woke up on Sunday morning, she knew at once that the persuading stick was calling to her. She could hear its silent music and smell that elusive fragrance that wasn't a smell at all. She left the drawer firmly closed, and stayed away from her bedroom all day. Aunt Jenny and Uncle Keith came, and after tea they all went to the park and played ball—all except Donald, who got up in midafternoon and went out.

Sarah cheered up, and ran around laughing with the rest. She forgot about the persuading stick. But at bedtime, when she went into her room, a vibration like a very slight but pleasant electric shock ran through her, and the soundless music and odorless scent poured from the closed drawer. When Mum came into the room, Sarah expected her to remark on them, but Mum said nothing and didn't seem to feel anything.

Alone again, Sarah found herself opening the drawer without having intended to. Her fingers found the stick at once. It seemed almost to have jumped into them. At once she felt peaceful and confident. She didn't know why she had been resisting the stick. It was a marvelous, a glorious thing. She took it to bed with her and slept with it under the pillow. And she had a night of dreaming. In the morning she didn't know what she'd dreamed about—she couldn't remember a thing—but she knew her dreams had been happy. After breakfast she put the stick in her Winnie the Pooh pencil case, where it just fitted, and took it to school with her.

Sarah was in Class 4F. It was called 4F because the teacher was Mrs. Freedman. There were also 4C, taught by Mrs. Cary, and 4W, taught by Mr. Williams. Of the three, 4F was the naughtiest and the noisiest. Everybody said so, especially Mrs. Freedman. Mrs. Freedman said that in all her twenty-two years of teaching she'd never had a class as naughty and noisy as the present 4F. Beth was sure Mrs. Freedman said that every year, but Ron Berry and Derek Curtis took her remark as special praise and went round the school boasting of it.

This morning, perhaps because it was Monday and a fine day and nobody wanted to be in school, 4F was naughtier than usual. There was a lot of whispering and shuffling, and some of the bigger boys were tormenting their neighbors and getting told to stop it. Mrs. Freedman herself was in a cross mood. In the end she announced that she was going to keep 4F in for the first five minutes of playtime. And when there were complaints from Ron Berry and Derek Curtis and Jason Sellars, she was so cross she made it the first ten minutes of playtime instead of five.

So when the bell rang, 4F sat furiously at their tables while Mrs. Freedman marked some books. And Beth leaned across to Sarah and whispered, "Have you got that stick?"

Sarah didn't answer but nodded.

"Persuade her to let us go!" whispered Beth.

"Be quiet, Beth!" called Mrs. Freedman.

Beth waited a minute, then whispered again, more quietly, "Go on! Persuade her!"

And Sarah felt the persuading stick calling to her. She felt that it wanted to be used, and that she wanted to do what it wanted. She took the stick from her pencil case and held it in one hand, concealed by her sleeve, while she raised the other hand.

It was a minute or so before Mrs. Freedman noticed that Sarah had her hand up. Then she said wearily, "Yes, Sarah, what is it?"

Sarah said, "Please, Mrs. Freedman, let us go now."

Mrs. Freedman stared.

"What?" she asked, astonished.

"Please, Mrs. Freedman, let us go out and play."

"Certainly not!" said Mrs. Freedman. "Not until ten minutes are up."

Without knowing what made her do it, Sarah got up from her seat and walked to the front of the class. She looked Mrs. Freedman in the eye. In her hand, the persuading stick felt alive and alert. Mrs. Freedman said, "Sarah! How dare you?" Then she hesitated. In a different tone of voice she said, "Well, Sarah, perhaps I was a bit hasty. Perhaps just this once I could . . . Yes, I suppose so. You can all go out now."

Nobody waited to be told twice. There was a rush for the door, led by the big boys. Mrs. Freedman and Sarah were left looking at each other.

Mrs. Freedman said, weakly, "I suppose I thought I'd kept you in long enough." She sat down at her desk.

As when she'd used the persuading stick before, Sarah felt tired. She'd have liked to sit down, too.

"Go on, Sarah, out you go!" said Mrs. Freedman, and smiled feebly.

With an effort Sarah pulled herself together and went out into the playground. Several of her classmates gathered round her. Derek Curtis said admiringly, "That was neat!"

Ron Berry asked, "Did you *hypnotize* old Freezebum?"

Beth lined herself up with Sarah. "No!" she declared. "Sarah has a persuading stick!"

Ron said, "Tell me another one!" but Derek was interested.

"What's a persuading stick?" Derek asked.

"It's a kind of magic wand," said Beth.

Sarah shook her head fiercely. She didn't want the persuading stick talked about. Ron Berry jeered.

"Magic wand!" he echoed. "Sarah Casson has a magic wand! Who do you think you are, Sarah—the Fairy Queen?"

Sarah was silent. Beth said, "It works! She can persuade anybody to do anything!"

"Make me jump over the school, then!" said Ron Berry.

"It won't make you do anything you *can't* do," said Beth. "But it'll make you do anything you *can* do. Make me touch my toes, Sarah, like you did on Friday!"

Sarah didn't respond. Beth said, "Go on, show them! Make me touch my toes. Make *him* touch *his* toes!"

"I don't want to," said Sarah. "It makes me tired."

Ron said, "Ha, ha, ha!" in a loud, disbelieving voice, but Derek Curtis said, "Let's *see* the stick, Sarah!"

Ann Peters said, "Go on, Sarah. Show us!"

"I don't want to."

"Come on, Sarah! Let's have a look!"

Reluctantly, Sarah opened the pencil case and took out the persuading stick.

"Show us how it works!" said Derek.

They were all looking expectantly at Sarah. Beth said, "Go on, show them! They won't believe you unless you do!"

"Oh, go away!" Sarah said to Derek. She didn't mean to persuade him with the stick. But Derek looked at her with the puzzled expression that she'd now seen on half a dozen people's faces. Without a word, he headed away toward the far end of the playground. Then he turned and came back.

"I—I thought I'd left something over there," he said.

"You see?" said Beth triumphantly. "It works." She sounded as proud of the stick as if it were hers. She went on, "My turn now, Sarah."

"No," said Sarah. "There aren't any turns with this. It's mine."

Jason Sellars had been watching what went on without saying anything. He was the son of Mrs. Sellars, from whose garden Sarah had got the ball back. He wasn't like Mrs. Sellars to look at. He was podgy, whereas his mother was thin and angular. But he was like his mum in being unpleasant.

"Let *me* have a go!" he demanded now.

"No," said Sarah again.

"Come on. Just for a minute."

"No."

Jason wouldn't take no for an answer. He grabbed one end of the stick. Sarah clung for a moment to the other end. Then, afraid that the stick might break, she let go. And without the stick she instantly felt weak and without confidence. She even felt smaller.

Jason waved the stick in the air. "Abracadabra!" he said. "Stick, do your stuff. Sarah, stand on your head!"

For a few seconds Sarah just stood where she was. She didn't feel any urge to stand on her head. The stick wasn't working for Jason. It was silently calling to her from his hand. But she knew she wasn't strong enough to get it back. When she moved toward him, Jason fended her off with his free hand.

"I'll give it one more chance!" he said, waving the stick at Beth. "Beth Anderson, kick Sarah's bottom!"

"I won't!" said Beth.

"Katherine Wells, *you* kick Sarah's bottom," said Jason. "And Beth's as well!"

Katherine stood without moving.

"Well, go on!" said Jason. "Be persuaded. That's what the stick's supposed to do."

But Katherine still didn't move.

"See?" said Jason scornfully. "It doesn't work. Who do you think you're kidding, Sarah? It's only an old stick. Go and play with the babies! See if *they'll* believe you!"

"Give her the stick back, then!" said Beth. "It works for her."

Jason looked at the stick. He seemed on the point of handing it back. But he didn't. He said, "It's a nice bit of stick. I'll keep it."

"Oh, go on, give her the stick back!" said Derek Curtis.

Jason wouldn't. Suddenly Sarah had a strange sensation in her hand, as though the stick was in it, though actually it was still in Jason's. She took a deep breath and looked Jason in the eye.

"Jason Sellars," she said quietly, "give me that stick!"

For a moment Jason resisted. Everyone was looking at him. He scowled and clutched the stick as if it was trying to get away. Then he threw it, peevishly, in Sarah's direction. She stretched out a hand. Sarah wasn't very good at catching a ball, but she had no trouble with the stick. It flew neatly into her grasp.

"*I* don't want your old stick!" said Jason.

Mrs. Cary, who was the youngest teacher, was on playground duty. She walked close to the group. Sarah said, without knowing where the idea came from, "Jason Sellars. Go to Mrs. Cary and say, 'I am a big fat slob.' "

Jason reddened. "I—I'll . . ." he threatened, stepping toward Sarah as if he was going to hit her. Then he turned away and walked reluctantly toward Mrs. Cary.

"Do you want *me*, Jason?" she asked. "Come along, then. I won't bite you."

Jason looked shamefaced. He went slowly and painfully, as if forcing his way against the wind.

"Well, Jason. What is it, then?" Mrs. Cary asked. She smiled encouragingly.

"M-Mrs. Cary . . ." Jason began, and hesitated. Then the words all came out in a rush. "Mrs. Cary, I am a big fat slob!" And having said it, Jason rushed away, scarlet-faced.

Mrs. Cary's eyes followed Jason's departing form. She turned to the group of children.

"What*ever* made him say that?" she asked. "Was it a dare, or a forfeit, or something?"

None of the children answered. They didn't know what to say.

"Oh, well, never mind!" said Mrs. Cary. She was smiling. Sarah wondered for a moment if Mrs. Cary thought that what Jason had said about himself was all too true.

Then the bell rang for the end of playtime. The persuading stick felt dead in Sarah's hand now, and she was wearier than ever before. She slid the stick back into her Winnie the Pooh pencil case and moved with the others toward the school door. Her legs were so weak they would hardly carry her.

5

Going into the classroom, the other children made way for Sarah. She was something of a heroine. She had won back their playtime and she had made Jason Sellars look foolish. They'd enjoyed seeing that. Nobody liked Jason Sellars. But Sarah didn't feel like a heroine. She'd begun the day feeling strong and happy, but the use of the persuading stick had drained the strength and joy out of her. She dragged her way to her chair and slumped down on it.

Her own eyes drawn to Sarah by those of the class, Mrs. Freedman looked at her with concern.

"Is there something wrong, Sarah?" she asked.

"No, Mrs. Freedman," Sarah said.

Susie Barnes, the youngest child in the class, blurted out, "She's got a magic wand!"

Several people said "Ssssh!" They had a feeling that the less teachers were told about such things, the better. But Mrs. Freedman had heard.

"A magic wand?" she inquired. "What *is* all this about?"

Sarah didn't answer. She was so tired that for the moment she didn't care about anything. She cupped her face between her hands and put her elbows on the table.

Mrs. Freedman, who was a strict teacher, didn't allow that. She told Sarah to sit up straight. "And now," she said, "will somebody *please* tell me what is going on?"

"She has a magic wand," repeated Susie Barnes. "She has, really!"

Mrs. Freedman, who had been frowning, smiled.

"Well, well," she said. "So Sarah has a magic wand. How interesting. What game were you playing?"

"It wasn't a game, it was *real!*" said Susie.

"It couldn't have been *real*, dear," said Mrs. Freedman to Susie, gently. "There aren't such things as magic wands in real life. But it must have been a very interesting game. Tell us more about your magic wand, Sarah. And may we all have a look at it?"

"It's just a piece of stick," said Sarah desperately.

"Let me see it, all the same," said Mrs. Freedman. Her voice was calm, but there was a steely note in it that the class knew well. "Bring it to me at once!" she said to Sarah.

It was no use arguing. Reluctantly, Sarah opened her pencil case and took out the stick. Mrs. Freedman held out her hand for it. Sarah walked to the front of the class and put it in Mrs. Freedman's hand. It felt quite dead now.

Mrs. Freedman studied the stick.

"An interesting color and texture," she said. "It's hollow, isn't it? And"—she bent the ends of the stick toward each other with her hands—"slightly springy. Where did you find it, Sarah?"

"In a clump of stalks," said Sarah, "on the canal bank."

"Well, it doesn't look to me like anything that could have been *growing*," said Mrs. Freedman. "I'd have said it was man-made. A piece of tubing of some kind, I think, though I haven't seen anything like it before. However, I suppose it might just about pass muster as a magic wand. I hope you're not going to turn me into a frog, Sarah."

"Oh, no," said Sarah. "It doesn't do things like that."

"Well, that's a relief," said Mrs. Freedman. "I think I'll take charge of it for the time being, just to be on the safe side." She put it in her desk. "You can sit down now, Sarah. And, class, arising out of that, I have a nice project for you. I shall be busy for the rest of the morning, so I want you to get on with it quietly. I want you all to write me an essay called, 'If I Had a Magic Wand.' You can tell me what you would do with such a thing."

Sarah was feeling more like herself by now. She started writing along with the others. "If I had a magic wand," she wrote, "I would magic a big new house for my mum and dad, with double glazing. I would magic two new cars for them and a motorbike for my brother Donald, and they would be specially safe, so that nobody could have accidents with them."

She paused and considered. "I would magic myself beautiful," she added. It was quite an interesting game, though she didn't feel it had any connection with the persuading stick. By the time the morning was over, she had magicked a large increase of income and lots of expensive clothes for her family; then, turning to a wider stage, she had made everybody in the world kinder to everybody else and had had a peace treaty signed by all nations that would last forever.

The bell rang for the end of morning school as Mrs. Freedman was collecting the essays. "I shall look forward to reading these," she said. And as Sarah filed out, Mrs. Freedman called her back.

"Do you want your *actual* magic wand, Sarah?" she inquired. She lifted her desk lid and held out the stick.

But Sarah hadn't liked the tiredness that followed when she used the stick. She was just a little afraid of it. She wouldn't have minded if Mrs. Freedman had forgotten to give it to her.

"I don't want it back, Mrs. Freedman," she said. Mrs. Freedman looked surprised, and Sarah added, "Truly I don't."

"Oh, come now, take it, Sarah. It really is rather nice, whatever it is. Do take it."

As Mrs. Freedman spoke, Sarah felt in her mind that the stick wanted her to take it. And she was helpless to resist. Just as her legs had felt like water at the end of playtime, her mind felt like water now. She was being persuaded. By Mrs. Freedman or by the stick? Or by something inside herself? She didn't know, but she watched her hand go out in front of her and take the persuading stick from the teacher. It settled into her hand as if it was taking possession.

"Th-thank you, Mrs. Freedman," she stammered, and ran from the room.

In the lunch line, Wayne Griggs, who was a thin boy but very greedy, whispered to Sarah to persuade the serving lady to give him an extra sausage. Sarah took no notice. One thing she was sure of was that she wasn't going to use the persuading stick to get sausages for Wayne Griggs. In fact she still didn't want to use it at all.

After lunch she took refuge in the library, sitting down at the table farthest from the door with a book picked at random from the shelves. Quite a number of children came in to choose books, but the day was so fine that almost nobody wanted to stay indoors, and only two others settled down in the library to read. One was Emma Radley, who was always reading. The other was Jason Sellars. Sarah looked at Jason with alarm. He couldn't touch her while they were under the eye of the librarian, Mrs. Hughes, but she didn't know what he might do to her out of school. Jason was a bully.

Jason didn't look furious or threatening, though. He looked embarrassed. He also looked a little afraid of Sarah, as if she might tell him to repeat his earlier performance.

"It's a surprise to see *you* in here, Jason," Mrs. Hughes said when she had a quiet moment. "And fancy finding you reading this!"

Jason had a book on Roman Britain in front of him. Sarah guessed that he'd chosen it as much at random as she'd chosen hers.

"Are you finding it interesting, Jason?" Mrs. Hughes went on.

Jason blushed. "Yes, Mrs. Hughes," he said, looking at the floor. Then two children went up to the counter with books they wanted to borrow, and Mrs. Hughes went to attend to them. Jason gave Sarah a sickly grin, followed by two or three more such grins before the bell rang for afternoon school. Sarah pretended not to notice. She was relieved that he hadn't hissed "Just you wait!" at her, but she didn't much want him to be friendly, either.

Neither of them actually said anything. Emma Radley was so engrossed in her book that she didn't hear the bell, and Mrs. Hughes had to turn her out.

All through afternoon school, Sarah was aware of the persuading stick in her pencil case. She could hear, very faintly, its silent music, and felt that it was appealing to her to be taken out. But she didn't open the case. As soon as school ended, she picked up the case, crammed it into her shoulder bag, and rushed away home before anyone could stop her. She went straight to her room, put the stick in her dressing table, and shut the drawer on it with a sense of relief.

She went downstairs to find a scene going on in the kitchen between Donald and Mum. Donald looked all scruffy and crumpled, as if he hadn't been out of bed long. He was sitting at the kitchen table with a mug of tea in front of him, smoking a cigarette. Mum was standing at the sink with her hands on her hips, looking very cross and very determined.

"I will *not*," she was saying, "have your room left in such a state!"

Donald said wearily, "What're you worrying for? You don't have to go in it. Just keep the door closed and forget it."

"How can I forget it?" Mum demanded. "It's not sanitary. Cigarette ends everywhere and dirty clothes on the floor and the bed never made . . ."

"It's me that has to live in it," said Donald. "Not you."

"Well, *I*'m not going to clean it up, I can tell you that. Not when you're at home all day, doing nothing."

"Nobody asked you to clean it up," said Donald. He drew on his cigarette and puffed out smoke.

"This is my house," said Mum, "or rather, it's your dad's and mine, and I won't have a room in it left in that disgusting condition!"

"So what're you going to do about it?" inquired Donald.

"I shall talk to your father when he comes home."

"Okay," said Donald. "You do that. I won't be here. I'm going round to Gemma's."

He stubbed out his cigarette, shoved the mug away from him, and sloped off out of the room.

On the way out, he paused for a moment, as he always did, to rumple Sarah's hair.

"Hi there, Tiddles," he said. "How's things?"

"Don't call me that. I keep telling you."

"And I keep forgetting. Sorry, Sarah. I'm in trouble with everyone these days, aren't I? Even you."

Sarah would have liked to tell Donald he was never in trouble with her. She'd looked up to him since she was tiny, and although she was old enough now to know that he wasn't perfect, the way she felt about him hadn't really changed. But Donald didn't wait for her to say anything. After the scene with Mum, it seemed he couldn't get out of the room quickly enough.

Mum was silent when Donald had gone. She went about her work slowly and thoughtfully, with a frown on her face. She didn't ask Sarah, as she usually did, what sort of a day she'd had at school. And when Robin came in, ten minutes later, she hardly looked up.

"The kids in your class are all talking about you," Robin told Sarah. "They say you've got a magic wand or something."

Sarah pretended not to hear.

"What are they talking about?" Robin continued.

Sarah still wouldn't answer him. Robin turned to

Mum. "The kids are saying our Sarah has a magic wand," he told her.

"A what?" said Mum. "Oh, a magic wand. How nice." She wasn't attending. "I really don't know what I'm going to do about that boy," she said, meaning Donald. "As for you two, you can have a chocolate biscuit each, and why don't you go out and play until supper time?"

Robin followed Sarah outside. His curiosity wasn't satisfied. He crammed his biscuit into his mouth, chewed, and swallowed rapidly. Then he said, "They say you make people do things they don't want to do. They say you made Jason Sellars call himself a fat slob." He giggled. "Wish I'd heard him. He *is* a fat slob." Then, "You can't do it *really*, can you? You just make them *think* you can."

Sarah still said nothing. Robin went on, "Show me the wand!"

"I haven't got it," said Sarah.

"Where is it?"

"I put it somewhere."

"Go and get it."

"No."

"Oh, go *on*." Then, a moment later, "I know why you won't. Because it's just an old stick you picked up. Anybody can pick up an old stick and pretend it's a magic wand."

"Then why are you interested?"

"I'm *not* interested," said Robin. "If you won't

even show me the stick, that *proves* it's all rubbish."

He picked up his tennis ball from the grass and began hitting it against the wall of the house. But there was a puzzled look on his face. After a couple of minutes he caught the ball in midbounce.

"Did you use your stick on Mrs. Sellars the other day?" he inquired.

"If it's rubbish, I couldn't have done, could I?" Sarah retorted.

"No. 'Course not," said Robin. He shook his head, as if to dismiss the whole idea of magic wands, and went on with his wall tennis.

Half an hour later, rain drove them indoors. There was nothing worth watching on television, and they started a game of Monopoly, setting out the board on the carpet in a corner of the sitting room. They continued after supper, and were still playing when Mum and Dad came in.

Usually Mum and Dad didn't talk about Donald in front of the younger children. But they were worried about him, and today they couldn't keep off the subject. And Sarah and Robin seemed to be fully occupied with their game.

"If this goes on much longer," Mum said, "somebody's going to be driven crazy. And I know who it'll be."

"It's just a phase. He'll be different when he gets a job."

"If and when," said Mum. "He isn't even trying."

"There aren't many jobs around," Dad remarked.

"If he'd only behave like a human being living with other human beings, I could stand it," Mum said. "But he gets worse. He doesn't even pretend to show any consideration. And as for that room of his . . . it's unspeakable."

"He's a good boy at heart," said Dad. "He's having a hard time."

"It's all very well for you to be sympathetic, Trevor. You're out at work all day. But I have him all the time, when he isn't lying in bed smoking—and as for that, he'll be setting his bedclothes on fire one of these days. One way and another, it's getting to be more than I can take!"

Mum's voice was rising, and Robin and Sarah were listening, though they didn't look up. Dad gave Mum a meaningful glance, as if to say, "Not in front of the children." Mum was quiet for a minute. But she was all worked up, and it wasn't long before she began again.

"I think that girl's responsible for a lot of it."

"Who? Gemma?" asked Dad.

"Yes, of course, Gemma. That pipsqueak. He was all right until he took up with her. At least, he was better than he is now. He's obsessed with her."

Dad said, "Don't you think he *needs* a girlfriend? No job, not much money . . . It isn't much of a life for a lad his age."

"I don't mind him having a girlfriend. Of course I don't. But that one . . . She's still at school, believe it or not, but from the way she looks and behaves, you'd think . . . well, I don't know *what* you'd think."

"Now, now!" said Dad. "Isn't it time we talked about something else?"

"Gemma's going to ditch him," said Robin casually.

"You weren't supposed to be listening to this conversation," said Dad.

"I couldn't help it, could I?" said Robin.

"Anyway, who told you that?" demanded Mum.

"Warren told me. He should know, shouldn't he? He's her brother. She's going to drop our Donald. She's got a new guy. Donald doesn't know yet."

"Well, if that was true," said Mum, "it'd be the best news for months. But Warren's only your age. I expect he's got it wrong. Donald's out with Gemma this evening."

"Warren always knows about Gemma's boyfriends," said Robin.

"It would be nice if he was right about this," Mum said.

"Nice for who?" said Dad. "What do you think the effect would be on Donald?" And then, glancing at the two children in the corner of the room, "Let it drop for now. Isn't there *anything* on TV?"

All through an evening spent watching television, Sarah worried about Donald. She didn't like Donald to be unhappy and she didn't like him to be at odds with her parents. After she'd gone to bed she lay awake, still worrying about him. When he came in, late, she heard his raised voice and those of her parents, arguing for ten or fifteen minutes. Then she heard Donald's footsteps coming upstairs in a rush, and the slam of his bedroom door.

And still she couldn't sleep. Hours seemed to go by. Then she began to hear, quite low, the silent music of the persuading stick, calling from the closed drawer.

During the day, she'd gone off the persuading stick. She hadn't liked the tiredness and the sense of unease that came over her when she used it. For a while she resisted opening the drawer. But the music grew more insistent, and she remembered that the previous night she'd slept beautifully with the stick under her pillow.

In the end she couldn't fight it any longer. She got out of bed and padded to the drawer. Once again the stick seemed to jump into her hand. She put it under her pillow, and went to sleep at once.

She didn't sleep quite as well as she had the night before. A note of anxiety ran through her dreams, and although she couldn't remember any of them in the morning she had a faint recollection that they were all to do with Donald.

6

Next morning, Sarah found it hard to get out of bed. She wasn't fully rested, and still felt half asleep and under the influence of the persuading stick. Without really intending to, she took the stick from under her pillow and put it in her pencil case. But by the time she arrived at school, she was wide awake and had decided she didn't want to use it.

At morning and afternoon playtime it stayed in her pencil case. At lunchtime, she went straight from the dining hall to the library. She put her shoulder bag under the table, between her feet. She couldn't hear the silent music now, but she was very conscious of the stick, imprisoned in her bag. A feeling like a slight electric current, quite painless, ran through her feet and partway up her legs.

After school, Sarah stayed on in the classroom as long as she could. She didn't want anyone urging her to use the stick. When Mrs. Freedman turned her out, she moved as slowly as possible, hoping that everyone would have gone home. But no. Beth and Katherine were waiting for her. And with them was Jason Sellars.

Jason was still in a would-be friendly mood. He hung on to the little group and wouldn't go away, although they talked only to one another and not to him.

On the way home they had to pass Mrs. Goodier's little shop. Jason edged his way into the group and dug Sarah in the ribs.

"Hey, Sarah!" he said. "Make Goody Goodier give us all ice creams!"

Sarah opened her mouth to say "No," but the word didn't come out. She didn't want to use the persuading stick, and at the same time she wanted very much to use it. She felt her hand straying to her shoulder bag, taking out the pencil case. Everybody watched. The children gave a little gasp as the persuading stick came into view. They all craned to see it, though it lay there as quietly as a pencil. None of them seemed to hear or feel anything, but the stick was singing silently to Sarah, wanting her to use it.

She took it from the pencil case, and it settled into her fingers. She felt powerful, and she wanted to show her power. She could tell anybody to do anything and they would do it. She could have told the children to walk on past Mrs. Goodier's. But that wouldn't have satisfied her. Now that she had the stick in her hand, she wanted to make an impression.

"All right," she said. "Come on."

In a little gang they trooped into Mrs. Goodier's shop. There was nobody else there. Mrs. Goodier didn't do much business these days. Everybody went to the big, bustling newsagent's shop that had opened on the Parade, and that sold sweets and cigarettes and all sorts of other things besides newspapers. Mrs. Goodier was old and slow, and took her time. Now she came shuffling out from the back of the shop.

"Mrs. Goodier," said Sarah, "I want you to give us all an ice cream. Free." She gulped. "Big ones. Rainbow cornets."

Rainbow cornets were the most expensive. Mrs. Goodier stared. Sarah felt the persuading stick move like a live thing in her hand. Then Mrs. Goodier shuffled to the freezer and took out four of the big multicolored cornets. With a bemused expression, she handed them out to the children. Jason disappeared from the shop at once with his cornet. The others stood there, feeling awkward.

Katherine groped in her bag. She knew what a rainbow cornet cost. She offered the money to Mrs. Goodier. But Mrs. Goodier, still looking baffled, refused it.

"No," she said. "I *gave* you them." A pause. "Didn't I?"

Neither Beth nor Sarah had the money to pay for a rainbow cornet anyway. The three of them, still feeling awkward, walked out of the shop. Sarah was weak in the legs as well as embarrassed. She sat down on a low wall, a few yards farther along the street. The others joined her, including Jason, whose cornet was half eaten already.

"That was great!" he said. "You could do it every day!"

But Katherine said, "She's a poor old lady. She can't afford to give ice creams away."

Sarah felt ashamed of what she'd done. She put the persuading stick back in her pencil case, and the pencil case in the shoulder bag. Somehow she didn't fancy her rainbow cornet.

"I don't think I want this ice cream," she said.

"If you don't want it, I'll have it," said Jason, who was just swallowing the last of his.

"No, you won't," said Beth. She hadn't unwrapped her cornet. Neither had Katherine or Sarah. Beth collected the three of them and, without saying a word, took them back to Mrs. Goodier's shop.

"She didn't know what had happened," Beth said when she came back. "She was all confused. But they're back in the freezer now. All but Jason's."

"They were *your* ice creams," said Jason. "She gave them to you."

"I *made* her give them to us," said Sarah. "That's not the same."

"You must be bonkers," said Jason. "Free ice creams, and you give them back!"

"Get lost, Jason Sellars!" said Beth.

But Jason still hung around. Sarah couldn't stand the sight or sound of him. Wearily she reached for the persuading stick. "Go on. Off you go!" she said. Jason looked for a moment as if he was going to argue. But his eyes were on the stick, and he gave up without a struggle and trudged away.

Getting rid of Jason had taken the last bit of Sarah's energy. She sat on the wall for a long time before she felt strong enough to walk home. Beth and Katherine sat with her. They were all rather quiet. As they parted, Katherine said, "I don't think I like that stick."

Beth was more thoughtful than usual, too. She said, "You could do awful things with it. What if someone nasty had it?"

Sarah said, "I think it only works for me." But she wasn't at all sure.

When she got home, she put the stick in her drawer. Her hand was reluctant to let it go. It was an effort to open her fingers, and it was another effort to get her hand out of the drawer. It was a relief to slam the drawer shut and feel free.

On top of the dressing table was a little box with money in it that she'd been saving to buy a birthday present for Dad. She took thirty-five pence from it and went back to Mrs. Goodier's shop, where she put the money on the counter and ran away quickly before the old lady appeared. That was to pay for Jason's ice cream. But she still felt uneasy. She was afraid of the power the persuading stick had.

Arriving home once more, Sarah put her head round the kitchen door.

"Hello, Mum," she said.

Mum was sitting at the table, her head cupped between her hands. She smiled wearily at Sarah, but didn't get up.

"Get yourself some milk and a biscuit if you want," she said.

"Are you all right, Mum?"

"I'm all right," said Mum. But she didn't sound as if she really meant it.

Sarah sniffed the air. There was a smell of cigarette smoke. Donald had been in the kitchen. That would be why Mum had her head in her hands. There'd been another row.

"I don't want anything, thank you," Sarah said. She went out of the house, and for a minute or two she watched Robin, who was playing his endless game of wall tennis. As she watched, a thought occurred to her that made her heart bump. She could use the stick to make Donald tidy his room. If he was like all the other people she'd persuaded, he wouldn't know afterward why he'd done it. It would please Mum and make things easier in the house.

But she didn't want to do it. A few minutes ago she'd been thankful to put the stick away. The thought of it, lying in wait in her drawer, frightened her afresh. Not even to settle a row in the house did she want to get it out.

And yet . . . at the same time, there was something in her that *did* want to use the stick, and wanted very much to use it. She found herself going into the house again, walking upstairs, pushing open the door of her room. In spite of her fright, she was opening the drawer and the stick was in her hand.

The door to Donald's room was half open. Sarah tapped on it. Donald was lying on his bed.

"Come in!" he called.

Sarah went into the room. It smelled of unmade bed and dirty clothes and stale cigarette smoke. Poor Donald, she thought; and, thinking about him, she thought less about the stick.

"How's it going, Tiddles?" Donald inquired. Sarah looked at him and he added hastily, "I mean Sarah."

"Oh, all right," Sarah said. "How's things with you?"

"Lousy. What d'you want an elder brother for, Sarah? If I was you I wouldn't. Not if the elder brother was me."

"I do want you," said Sarah. As she spoke, it came over her once more that she loved Donald dearly. Maybe she loved him even more than she loved the rest of her family. And Donald was so sad these days. She felt the tears come into her eyes. She went toward Donald, wondering whether she dared kiss him. He might turn away from her, and that would hurt.

Donald noticed the tears.

"Hey, Sarah, pet," he said. "What have *you* got to be upset about?"

"I don't like it when you're not happy," Sarah said.

"Come off it. It's not your fault that I'm like what I'm like. Cheer up. Here"—he groped in his pocket—"get yourself an ice cream."

Sarah was hurt. "You think I'm still a little kid," she said, "that you can make happy with an ice cream?"

"There, there," said Donald. "Sorry, sorry, sorry. I should have realized how grown up you are now. Well, Sarah, anything I *can* do to cheer you up?"

"You could tidy your room," said Sarah firmly.

Donald's expression changed. "Mum's been getting at you!" he said.

"She hasn't. I thought of it myself."

"Why should you care? Why should anybody care? What's it matter to anyone? I'm the one who has to live in it."

"It matters to Mum," said Sarah. "She can't bear it."

"It's a power struggle," said Donald. "Now listen to me. You're telling me not to treat you as a little kid. I'm not to call you Tiddles. Well, all right, Sarah. Try and understand. I've got nothing, see? Mum and Dad keep me. I'm a nonpaying lodger. They pay the piper, so they want to call the tune. It's natural enough. I don't blame them. But I've got to have *some* independence, Sarah. If I don't control my own room, I don't control anything. It's a matter of pride. A matter of self-respect, you could call it. You understand, Tiddles—I mean Sarah?"

Sarah thought for a minute. Then she said, "No, I don't understand. If it's your own room and you're in charge of it, that doesn't stop you keeping it clean."

Donald said, "I can't give way. It'd be letting them order me around, and I'm not having that. They wouldn't treat me like this if I was working."

Sarah said, "I think you're crazy, Donald Casson. If I was you, I'd clean it up because it's a mess, not because I'd been told to."

"You *are* getting to be a grown-up Tiddles."

Sarah had a brainwave. "Donald," she said, "*I'll* clean your room!"

Donald was startled. He said, "No, you won't. You're not a servant."

Sarah said, "I don't want to do it as if I was a servant. I want to do it because I . . ."

She paused. She was too embarrassed to say what she wanted to say. Yet Donald knew.

"Oh, Tiddles!" he said. He got off the bed. "Come here!" He hugged her. "I sometimes think you're the only person in the world that cares about me. Apart from Gemma, that is."

Sarah remembered that Robin had said Gemma was going to drop Donald. It seemed that Donald didn't know about that yet. It might not be true, of course. Anyway, what Donald had said was all wrong.

"We *all* care about you, Donald," she said. "Mum and Dad and Robin and me. We all do."

Donald gave a deep sigh. "Yeah, I know you all do really," he said. "I'm trying to tell you how I *feel* sometimes. Oh, Tiddles, if I was you, I wouldn't think much of *me*. No, I won't let you clean my room. You couldn't, anyway. Look at the state it's in."

The persuading stick was in Sarah's jeans pocket.

With its help, she thought, she could persuade Donald to let her clean his room. But he wouldn't *like* that. He would hate it. It would be better to make him do it himself. With her heart thumping, she clenched her fingers on the stick, and felt it respond to her pressure.

"Donald," she said, "*promise* me that you'll clean it!"

She looked straight into his eyes. Donald looked straight back at her. He said, reluctantly, "All right, seeing it's you. But it's not because I've been nagged into it. I *want* to clean it. It *is* getting into a mess. Time I did something."

The affection had gone from Donald's voice. "Satisfied? Off you go, then, Tiddles. Leave me to it."

He lit a fresh cigarette. Sarah couldn't stand cigarette smoke, and anyway she was tired out. She dragged herself across the landing to her own room. With enormous effort, she got the persuading stick into the drawer. Then she lay motionless on her bed until supper time.

At bedtime that night, the silent music began again. In spite of her fears, Sarah felt a powerful urge to get the stick out and put it under her pillow once more. But she resisted, and after a while the stick seemed to leave her alone. Then, tired after the previous restless night and the events of the day, she went to sleep. She woke up three or four times in the darkness, and each time she felt that vibrations were coming from the drawer, but she ignored them.

In the morning there was a sensation. Donald got up earlier than anyone else and cleaned out his room. He did it rapidly and not very thoroughly, but he did it. All he would say to Mum before going back to bed was, "Sarah persuaded me."

Mum was puzzled but delighted. "You must have some secret that I don't have," she said to Sarah.

Sarah wondered for a moment whether to tell Mum about the persuading stick, but decided not to. There wasn't any point, she thought. No grown-up would believe in such a thing.

7

Sarah didn't take the persuading stick to school on either of the next two days. Nobody asked her to produce it. Most of the children had either lost interest by now or decided that what happened in the playground on Monday was a trick or a game. Not even Beth or Katherine had anything to say about the stick. Sarah thought they were probably a little frightened of it, and not too keen to see it again, because they didn't know what it might do next.

On Wednesday afternoon, Mrs. Freedman asked some of the class to read aloud their essays on what they would do with a magic wand. Sarah's wasn't one of those read aloud. The best one, according to Mrs. Freedman, was by Emma Radley. Emma had used her imaginary magic wand to convert a riding-school pony into a white winged horse, on which she had ridden through the skies to a castle where a wicked enchanter had imprisoned a beautiful princess. Emma had freed the princess, and as a result had been invited to stay as often as she wished in the princess's golden palace. Mrs. Freedman said this showed an active imagination, unlike the efforts of some whose thoughts could not rise above houses and cars.

Afterward, at afternoon playtime, Jason Sellars came up to Sarah with a smirk on his face and tried to interest her in a scheme for using the stick to get free sweets and comics. Sarah sent him packing. Apart from this, there was no further mention at school of the persuading stick.

But the stick was worrying Sarah more and more. When she came into the house at teatime she could feel its vibrations even before she went upstairs. That night it called silently to her from the drawer, and again she wouldn't take it out, although a part of her wanted very much to do so. She found it much harder than it had been the previous night to close her mind to the stick and go to sleep. When at last she did sleep, it was only in fits and starts, and she woke time after time to feel the silent vibrations of the stick, imprisoned in its drawer.

On Thursday morning, Mum said, "You look peaky, Sarah. I hope you're not sickening for something."

Sarah said, "I'm all right, Mum. Don't fuss."

"Are you getting proper sleep?"

"Yes. 'Course I am."

"Are you eating your school lunches?"

"Yes, I am."

"Well, you're not eating much breakfast. Why don't you have a piece of toast?"

"I don't *want* a piece of toast."

"Children!" said Mum. "I sometimes think I can't do anything with any of you!"

On Thursday evening, while the rest of the family were at the supper table, Donald burst into the house. He was white-faced and wild-eyed.

"Well, that's it!" he declared. "It's all over! Finished! *Everything*'s finished! I'm telling you, it's the end!"

"Whatever's happened?" demanded Mum.

"She's been two-timing me, the little so-and-so! She said she was going to her gran's tonight, and she's out with Rick Harker! I *saw* them going into the Rialto! If I'd seen them ten seconds sooner I'd have knocked his teeth in!"

"Oh, my dear, I *am* sorry!" said Mum.

But Dad said, "Oh, come off it, lad. You're not the first person who's ever been let down like that.

It's not the end of the world. If that's how she's going to behave, you're well rid of her!"

Donald glared at his father. "What's the use of telling you *anything*?" he demanded, and flung out of the room, banging the door behind him.

Mum looked at Dad crossly.

"What's become of all the sympathy you had for him?" she asked. "Talking to him like that isn't any help at all. You say he needs a girlfriend, and then you tell him he's better off without her. Honestly, Trevor!"

Dad said, "He can find another. He's better off without that one. And I can't stand him when he starts dramatizing like that. It's time the lad learned some sense!"

Robin said, "Gemma was going to tell him. Warren said so. She couldn't get round to it. She thought he'd take it badly."

"She was right about that!" said Mum grimly. "Trevor, I'm worried about that boy, really worried. I'm afraid he may do something silly. And if he feels he can't talk to his parents, what are we to do?" She turned to Robin and Sarah. "You two, why don't you go outside and play? It's a fine evening. And this isn't your worry. Donald will sort himself out. Go on, off you go!"

It wasn't dark yet. Robin returned to his wall tennis. He offered to play against Sarah, but Sarah declined. She wasn't in the mood for wall tennis. She stood for a while watching him as he tried to beat his record of two hundred and thirty-two bounces, but her thoughts were not on him or his game. They were on Donald. It was true, Donald couldn't talk to his parents these days. The only person he could talk to was Sarah herself.

Unwillingly, she dragged herself indoors. The call of the persuading stick was louder than ever. She had to fight with herself in order to go to Donald's room instead of her own. But she made it, and tapped on his door, softly at first, then more loudly.

"Go away!" came Donald's voice.

"It's me. Sarah. . . . Can I come in?"

"No, you can't."

"Donald, please let me."

"I said no."

Sarah was making no progress. But in her own room was the persuading stick. It was calling to her even as she called to Donald. With its aid she might be able to get Donald to let her in, get him to talk to her, get him to promise not to do anything rash. If he made a promise to her, he'd keep it, as he'd done over cleaning the room.

But . . . by now she dreaded the stick. It wasn't only the alarming tiredness that came over her whenever she used it. It was a feeling that each time she gave way to it she lost some independence. She grew weaker and the stick grew stronger. She couldn't think where it would end.

Then, as she struggled with herself, Donald's door opened.

"Come in, poppet," he said.

Sarah went into his room. Donald drew her onto the bed beside him, and put his arm around her. He still looked tense, but he was calmer than he'd been when he first came into the house, and his tone was affectionate.

"You're a good little Tiddles," he said. "I mean, a good big Sarah."

"Donald," she said, "Mum thinks you might do something silly. What does she mean?"

"Oh, I dunno, Sarah. Nothing, really."

"Does she mean you might fight Rick Harker?"

"What, me fight that wimp? No, I won't do that. Mind you, like I said, when I saw them together I felt like knocking his teeth in. And I *could* do, too, but I've lost the urge. There's no point. It's *her* that's got the explaining to do. Her mum and dad'll be away this weekend, and I'm going round there on Saturday morning to have it out with her."

That sounded better than fighting. But Sarah was still alarmed.

"Donald, you wouldn't . . . you wouldn't do anything awful to *Gemma*, would you?"

Donald laughed, though he didn't sound amused.

"No," he said. "I won't lay a finger on her, I promise you that. Haven't you noticed, I never harm anybody but myself?"

Sarah heaved a deep sigh of relief. Donald said, "Now, off you go, Sarah. And stop worrying about me, won't you? I'm not worth worrying about." He lit a cigarette.

"You *are* worth worrying about," said Sarah, and went.

While she'd been in Donald's room, she hadn't been aware of the persuading stick at all. She hadn't tried to persuade Donald of anything—at least, not in so many words. But now she was outside his door she could sense it calling to her again. Had the stick had anything to do with Donald's assurances to her? She didn't know. And, when she came to think of it, his remark about only harming himself was not a comforting one. What did he mean by that?

It just wasn't possible to stop worrying. She was worried about Donald, and she was worried about the stick, and she didn't know which was worrying her more. She had an odd sense that the two were bound up together, though she didn't know why.

The night that followed was by far the worst she'd had. She lay awake hour after hour. The stick wouldn't leave her alone. Its call was no longer in the form of silent music. It was still soundless, yet it went through and through her head on a single note, like a whistle pitched so high that it couldn't be heard but could still be felt. It gave her a headache.

Halfway through the night she could stand it no more. She got out of bed and padded over to her dressing table. When she opened the drawer, the persuading stick seemed to leap into her hand. She got back into bed, put the stick under her pillow, and went straight to sleep. She dreamed and dreamed; and the dreams were all of being shut out of things. She was outside her own house, beating on the door, beating and beating in a panic, but nobody came to let her in. She was following Donald to a door in a wall, and Donald went through it, but it slammed in her face. She was going to school with Beth and Katherine. Beth and Katherine went into the school, and then the school vanished. There was no Beth, no Katherine, no school, only Sarah herself in the midst of nothing.

After one of these dreams, she cried out in terror. Then she was awake, and it was just getting light, and Mum was in the room with her. Mum stroked her forehead, which was all sweaty, and said, "You had a nightmare, my darling. What was it?"

"I was all on my own," said Sarah. But the dream was fading as she spoke, and that was all she could remember.

"Whatever it was," said Mum, "it wasn't real.

You're safe in your own home, and we're all here with you. There's nothing to worry about. Now go back to sleep."

"It was the stick," said Sarah.

"The what?"

"The stick!"

"What *are* you talking about?" said Mum. "Was that something in your dream?"

But Sarah was confused, and still only half awake. There weren't any vibrations coming from the stick now. She yawned. Mum said, "Now, back to sleep with you. No more bad dreams!"

Next time Sarah woke up, it was after nine o'clock. She ought to have been at school by now, but she'd been left to have her sleep out. The stick, beneath her pillow, seemed to have been sleeping, too. It still wasn't sending out any vibrations. Sarah left it where it was. She put on her dressing gown and slippers, and padded past Donald's closed door and down the stairs. Mum was sitting by herself at the kitchen table with a cup of coffee. Dad had gone to work and Robin to school.

Mum said, "Oh, there you are. You needn't have got up. How are you now? No more bad dreams, I hope." She sounded anxious.

Sarah said, "I'm all right."

Mum said, "You look peakier than ever. I've a good mind to take you to the doctor."

Sarah said crossly, "I tell you, there's nothing

wrong with me!" Then suddenly she burst into tears.

Mum put her arms round Sarah. "There, there," she said, and made comforting sounds. "What's the matter, my dear? Tell Mum all about it."

But Sarah could only sob.

Mum said, "You're worrying about Donald, aren't you? But you mustn't, darling. His troubles are for *him* to solve. And he *will* solve them, in time."

Suddenly Sarah knew she had to tell Mum everything, whether Mum believed it or not.

"It was all the persuading stick," she said. And out came the whole story. Mum listened, astonished.

"But, Sarah," she said at the end, "this stick can't *really* have been doing anything. You've done it all yourself. You can be *very* persuasive, my dear, in case you hadn't realized it."

"It *was* the stick," said Sarah. "And it sort of calls to me. I'm afraid of it. I feel as if I won't get rid of it, ever."

Mum said, "What nonsense! Where is it now, Sarah?"

"It's under my pillow."

"Go and fetch it, there's a good girl."

Sarah went upstairs and fetched the stick. It felt quite dead this morning, but she didn't trust it. It was almost as if it was lying low.

Mum picked it up and looked interestedly at its rough silveriness.

"It *is* a strange thing," she said. "And you found it in a clump of dead stalks? Well, it's hollow like a stalk, but I don't think it *is* a stalk, do you? I just don't know whether it's something natural or not."

Mum bent the ends toward each other, as Mrs. Freedman had done, and watched them spring back.

"You know what I'm going to do with this stick, Sarah?" she said. "I'm going to put it in the trash. Come and watch me."

Mum opened the kitchen door, took the lid off the trash can that stood outside, and dropped the stick in.

"So much for that!" she said.

She put the lid firmly back on the can. Sarah felt better and safer at once, as she'd done the first time she shut the stick away in her drawer. The stick hadn't shown any sign of life while Mum was handling it, and it wasn't calling to her now. She could almost feel the color coming back to her cheeks.

"Why, you look better already, Sarah!" said Mum. She went on, "Imagination is all very well, but sometimes it can take unhealthy forms."

"Mrs. Freedman thinks I haven't any imagination," said Sarah.

"Mrs. Freedman doesn't know you as well as I

do. Now, Sarah, I want you to put that thing right out of your mind. Will you do that? Promise?"

"I'll try," said Sarah.

"Good girl. Now, do you feel well enough to go to school? If you do, I'll take you. If you're not actually ill, I'd rather you were at school than hanging about and brooding at home."

Sarah felt the same. Her spirits had lifted. Mum had got rid of the stick in the most obvious way. It was a bit of junk, and she'd put it in the trash can, where it belonged. So much for that. Maybe, as Mum said, all the rest had been imagination. In that case, the whole affair was over now, and she was glad it was. If only Donald were happier, everything would be all right.

8

The rest of Friday went quite well—at least, during the daytime. The weather was fine. Mrs. Freedman was in a good temper. After school, Sarah walked home with Beth and Katherine, and they played together until bedtime. Robin spent the evening with Gemma's brother Warren; problems between Donald and Gemma made no difference to them. Donald stayed at home all evening. He shut himself in his room and played his music rather loudly, but this was what he usually did when he was at home. He turned it down when Sarah went to bed. And with the persuading stick out of the way, Sarah expected to go straight to sleep.

But it didn't work out like that. In spite of her relief, she found when she got into bed that she actually *missed* the stick. She could feel its absence from the drawer in which it usually sat. She missed the silent music that had appealed to her at first. The wish to have it under her pillow, which she'd resisted on the two previous nights, was as strong as ever.

Hour after hour went by. When Mum came in to kiss her good night, Sarah kept her eyes closed. Dad came into the room too, and Sarah heard Mum say, "I'm worried about this child, Trevor. We've had so much on our plates with Donald, we simply haven't given her the attention we should."

Dad said, "Sarah's all right."

Mum said, "She's been fantasizing about a magic wand or some such thing. And she's pale and peaky and off her food. I'm sure it's all because of Donald. She's so fond of him, and so sensitive."

"We mustn't talk about Donald in front of her," said Dad.

"No, of course not. Not a word from now on. But Donald himself doesn't make it easy . . ."

Sarah felt Mum's kiss, very light, on her forehead. Then Mum and Dad went out. Sarah still couldn't sleep. And soon she began to hear the persuading stick again. It was calling her from outside now. It was the soundless music, and she felt its attraction. She wanted very much to go downstairs and recover the stick. But she resisted the urge. Before long, the silent music changed to the single high continuous note, going through and through her head. Although it was silent, it seemed to get louder and louder inside her head, more and more piercing.

Sarah tiptoed to the bathroom. There was a roll of cotton wool there. She broke two buds off it and put them in her ears, but they didn't make any difference. The call grew louder still. She pulled the bedclothes up over her head and lay tossing, turning, squirming. In another minute she would have to cry out. Mum and Dad would come again, and in the morning they would take her to the doctor, and they would all be asking her questions she couldn't answer . . .

Then at last the call of the persuading stick faded and ceased. It seemed as if it had tired and was leaving her alone. She settled herself afresh, turned back the sheets, and went instantly to sleep.

In the morning she woke at her usual time. She felt fresh and rested and as though she'd had good dreams, though she couldn't remember them. And as soon as she was fully awake she realized that the persuading stick was in the room. And she knew where it was. She raised her pillow. The stick was underneath it.

She replaced the pillow quickly and climbed out

of bed, her heart thumping. How *could* the stick have got there? Could there be more magic about it than she knew of? It was terrifying. She picked it up and popped it in the drawer, handling it as if it was red hot though in fact it was cool to her touch and not showing any sign of life. She slammed the drawer shut, dressed quickly, and escaped from the room.

Donald's bedroom door was wide open. He was up and out already, hours before his usual time. Mum and Dad weren't up yet. They were having their Saturday lie-in. But Robin was in the kitchen, eating cornflakes. He looked at Sarah accusingly.

"What were you doing in the middle of the night?" he demanded.

Sarah stared. "What do you mean?" she asked.

"Walking round the house in your pajamas."

"I don't know what you're talking about."

"It's no good pretending. I *saw* you. I got up for the bathroom, and I was just going in when you came upstairs and went across the landing into your room. You pretended not to see me, but you must have done. And you had that stick in your hand!"

Sarah couldn't say a word. Robin said, as if struck by a sudden thought, "You weren't *sleepwalking*, were you?"

Sarah was still speechless. Robin said, in an awed tone, "You *were* sleepwalking!"

Sarah said, shakily, "I might have been."

"I'm going to tell Mum!" said Robin promptly.

"No, don't do that!"

"Why not? It's serious, sleepwalking. You might fall downstairs or something."

"I wouldn't."

"Well, I'm telling anyway."

Robin went on, in a reasonable tone, "It's not telling tales. Not when it's something that might hurt you. I've *got* to tell."

Sarah was confused. Everything was out of hand. Had she been sleepwalking? She would rather believe that than that the persuading stick had done something magic. Even so, the thought of sleepwalking was an alarming one. She said to Robin, "I don't think I was sleepwalking. Mum threw my persuading stick away. I went for it. I dare say I was half asleep."

Robin said, "You're bonkers. I keep telling you, it's just an old stick. You ought to be put away, you ought."

Sarah said nothing. She hoped Robin would drop the subject. Robin said, "If it really worked, you could use it on Gemma."

"How? Why?"

"You could persuade her to drop Rick Harker and go back to Donald."

"I don't know whether it would do that," said Sarah thoughtfully.

Robin hooted. " *'Course* it wouldn't do it. It

wouldn't do *anything*. But you believe in it, don't you? I keep telling you, you're bonkers. I *ought* to tell Mum and Dad. I ought to tell them, 'Our Sarah's round the twist. She believes in magic.' "

When Robin said that, Sarah knew he wouldn't tell their parents anything. She'd headed him off the subject of sleepwalking. He finished his cornflakes, picked up his tennis ball, and went outside. Sarah sat at the kitchen table, thinking hard.

Had she really been sleepwalking? Surely she hadn't. She remembered that she'd felt an enormous urge to go for the stick, just before she fell asleep. She must have done it while she was half asleep. There was all the difference in the world between doing something when you were half asleep and actually sleepwalking. The stick hadn't magicked itself into her room and she hadn't sleepwalked. She had fetched it herself. She was almost sure she could remember fetching it herself. Yes, she could remember opening the back door, feeling into the can, the stick jumping to her hand . . .

Jumping to her hand? That thought was frightening in itself.

Why had she gone to fetch the stick, when she wanted to be rid of it? Had the stick *made* her fetch it? Had it taken her over? What could she say to Mum now? Maybe Robin was right and she was bonkers.

Sarah got herself some juice from the fridge. As she was doing so, she heard sounds from above. Her parents were up and moving around. A minute later they both came into the kitchen.

"Well, there you are," said Mum. "I thought you might have slept a bit longer this morning." She looked at Sarah closely. "Are you feeling better today, my darling?"

Sarah said, "Yes, Mum."

"You still don't look too well. I'm not really happy about you. Perhaps you should see Dr. Lloyd after all. What do *you* think, Trevor?"

But before Dad had time to reply, the kitchen door flew open. Robin rushed in. Behind him, breathless, was Warren James. Warren stood gasping for breath. Robin said, "It's about our Donald!"

"Whatever . . . ?" began Dad.

Warren took two or three huge, gulping breaths. Then he said, "Donald's at our flat. On the balcony outside. Sitting on the rail." He gasped again. "He's threatening to throw himself off!"

"Oh, my God!" said Mum. Then, "Have you rung the police?"

Warren said, "No. We daren't. Donald says if he sees a policeman anywhere near, he'll jump."

9

Dad said, "I'm going up there!" and was out through the kitchen door almost before Warren had finished speaking. Mum stopped to think. When she spoke, her voice was quiet. But her body was tense, and she was gripping the back of the chair.

"This is real, is it, Warren?" she said. "It's not some horrible joke? Or Donald fooling?"

"It's real," said Warren. And nobody doubted him. They could tell from his face that it was real.

"Who's in the flat?" Mum asked.

"Only me and Gemma. My mum and dad are

away. There's only Gemma there now. And Donald."

"And what's it about?"

"It's about Rick Harker. There was a big row. Gemma said she was going with Rick now, and Donald was finished. And Donald said he'd jump."

Mum said in a steady voice, "I shall call the police, whatever he says. They'll find a way of getting there without being seen."

Warren said, "Can I go now, Mrs. Casson?"

Mum said, "That's up to you, Warren. But Robin and Sarah, you stay right where you are. Don't move from this kitchen."

Warren shot away at once. Mum went into the hall. They could hear her telephoning, but they couldn't hear what she said. It didn't take long. In half a minute, Mum was back. Her voice was still calm, but there was just a slight shake in it.

"I'm going over there," she said. "Now, listen to me. This is serious, but everything will be all right. You two are not involved. You must make yourselves some breakfast. You can play in the garden if you like. But you're not to come to Churchill Towers, understand?"

Sarah said, "B-but will Donald really jump off the balcony?"

Mum said, "No, of course he won't. He's upset, that's all."

Robin said, "If he did, he'd be killed. That

flat's on the fifteenth floor. It's *miles* to the ground."

Mum said, "Don't worry, it's not going to happen. But I'm not taking any chances. I shall go over there now. You just do as I say, and stay here. I'll let you know as soon as it's all over and Donald's come to his senses. He may have come in off the balcony already, I wouldn't be surprised."

Robin and Sarah, left together in the kitchen, stared at each other. Sarah was shocked and frightened. She felt as if she might be going to cry, but she was trying hard not to.

Robin surprised her. He put an arm round her shoulders. Robin never normally did that. "Don't worry, Sissy," he said. And "Sissy" was something he hadn't called her since she was little. "You heard what Mum said. It'll be all right."

He gulped. Sarah turned her head and looked into his eyes, and she could see that he was as frightened as she was. She held his hand.

For a minute or two, they sat silently together at the kitchen table. Then Robin said, "Sissy . . ."

"Yes?"

"Sissy, that stick . . ."

There were butterflies in Sarah's stomach.

"You think it persuades people, don't you?"

"I don't know," said Sarah. "I don't know what it does."

"Well, you've made people do things they didn't

want to. Like Jason Sellars calling himself a fat slob."

"I thought you didn't believe in it," said Sarah.

"I don't believe it's *magic*," Robin said, "But . . . well, if you could make people do things with it, it wouldn't matter whether it was magic or not, would it?"

Sarah said, "You mean . . . Donald?"

"Yes. 'Course I do."

Sarah felt terror deep inside her. A different kind of terror from the thought that Donald might jump from that balcony on the fifteenth floor of Churchill Towers. But terror all the same. By now she dreaded the stick.

Robin went on, "Did you have the stick when you persuaded him to clean up his room?"

Sarah nodded.

"Well, then, go and get it. And we'll get over there!"

"Mum told us to stay here."

"I know she did. I'm not deaf. But she can't stop us going. And if there's something you can do, we *ought* to go."

"They wouldn't let me," said Sarah. "They'd keep us away."

"Don't you want to try?"

Sarah thought of Donald, out on the balcony, fifteen stories up in the air. She thought of the look in Donald's eyes when he said she didn't need an elder brother like him. Of course she must go to Donald. Whatever Mum said, whatever anyone said, she must go to Donald.

And take the stick.

"Just a minute," she said. "I'll fetch it."

She went upstairs. At once she could feel the presence of the stick and hear its silent voice. It had never called to her so insistently. She felt sick inside, but she made herself go on. She pushed the bedroom door open.

The sound, the silent sound of the stick, was deafening. As soon as she went through the door she felt it pulling her toward it, as if it was a powerful magnet. She walked blindly to the dressing table. The top drawer seemed to open of its own accord, and the stick was in her hand.

Instantly the sound in her head switched off. The stick was speaking to her differently now. A warm tingle of power ran up from her hand, through her wrist and up her forearm. With the stick's help, she was strong. She could do anything.

She ran downstairs, holding it. She was powerful, powerful. Robin was waiting for her in the kitchen. She swept past him. "Come on if you're coming!" she called, but she knew it didn't matter whether Robin came or not.

She ran toward Churchill Towers. Robin ran after her, and usually he could ran faster than she could, but today she left him behind. The strength of the stick seemed to reach even to her legs.

It was less than half a mile to Churchill Towers, but it was all uphill. The Towers stood on the highest point for miles around. Sarah ran at top speed, but didn't feel tired or breathless. She was yards ahead of Robin when she reached the entrance.

It was quiet there. No sign of police or firefighters. You might have thought nothing was happening. But Sarah knew otherwise. The stick in her hand was urging her on, demanding to be used.

The elevator wasn't at the ground floor. But it was working. Lights flashed on its indicator. Sarah stood in front of it, suddenly breathless, urging it down toward her. "Come-on, come-on, come-on, come-on!" And then it was there. Nobody in it. Sarah flung herself in. She wasn't sure how to close the doors and set it moving. But Robin pounded up and got in after her, and Robin always knew about things like that. He pressed the right buttons, and in a moment they were soaring upward.

On the fifteenth floor, you could tell at once that something was happening. A knot of people had gathered outside the open doorway to one of the flats. That must be Gemma's. There was a buzz of low, excited conversation. Sarah walked toward the door, and was stopped by a man she didn't know.

"Go away, you kids!" he said. "It's nothing to do with you!"

"It's my brother!" Sarah hissed.

"You can't come in here!" the man said. But he looked uncertain. Sarah still felt full of power. She ducked swiftly under the man's arm. Somebody else moved toward her. She dodged, and was in through the door of the flat.

Along a short passage and into the main room. A largish sitting room. Three or four people in it. Two of them holding Gemma—Gemma wild-eyed, hair all over the place, sobbing loudly. At the window, their backs toward Sarah, not knowing she was there, Mum and Dad. At the outside of the window, just a shape, Donald.

Mum and Dad were talking to Donald through the open window. Urging. Arguing. Pleading. But there was no sound of Donald's voice. Sarah could only catch glimpses of him, because her parents were blocking the window.

Then Mum turned and saw her. She was furious. "Sarah!" she cried. "I told you not to come! Go back! Go back at once!"

Sarah heard her own voice saying loudly, "No, I won't!"

"I'm telling you! Go home!"

A man's arm went round her shoulders. It was the man who'd tried to stop her getting in. "I'll take her home," he was offering.

And then Donald's voice from outside the window, "Is that Sarah?"

The sound of his voice stopped everybody.

"That's the first thing he's said since we came," said Mum.

Sarah shouted, "Donald!" Then, with the words coming out as if somebody had put them there, "Donald! Talk to me!"

She was holding the persuading stick at her side. Nobody had noticed it. But it was throbbing in her hand. She pushed her way toward the window.

Donald said, "I'll talk to Sarah."

Dad said, "If you want to talk to Sarah, come inside." But Donald took no notice of that.

Sarah said quietly, "Let me go to him." Mum and Dad stepped aside. They looked bewildered. Somewhere in the room, Gemma sobbed. Sarah said, "Stop crying, Gemma, I can't hear." Gemma stopped crying.

Sarah went to the french window. Outside it was a tiny balcony, no more than three feet wide, with a waist-high railing around it. Donald was sitting perilously on a corner of the railing, smoking a cigarette. He grinned at Sarah, but his face was white.

"Just wanted to say goodbye, Tiddles," he said.

"You're not going anywhere," said Sarah.

"I am. Over the top. Don't you believe me?" Suddenly he swung round on his hands, so that his legs dangled over the balcony.

It looked as if he was about to jump. Mum, just behind Sarah, cried "No!" Donald looked over his shoulder. Sarah gazed steadily into his eyes but didn't say anything more. Donald swung his legs back and sat facing them.

"You see?" he said. "It's dead easy. Easy as falling off a log." He took both hands off the rail to get out a cigarette and light it. It was the last in the packet. Donald threw the packet over the rail.

"When this smoke's gone," he said, "I go, too."

Mum said, from behind Sarah, "Donald! How *could* you do that to the child?"

Donald's face froze. "If I got cross," he said, "I might go before."

The persuading stick tingled in Sarah's hand, still giving her power.

"You're not jumping at all, Donald," she said quietly.

"Who's stopping me?" asked Donald. Then, "Remember what I said the other day, Tiddles, I mean Sarah? What good's an elder brother like me? I'm useless, kid, useless. Two years out of school, never had a job, never done anything. No good to man or beast." He drew on the cigarette. "No good to her, neither. Prefers Rick Harker that works in a bank. I can't blame her, really. She's not been getting much from me lately. No fun at all. But she could have played straight. She could have *told* me she was going with him."

Mum said, "Maybe she was afraid something like this would happen."

Donald scowled. "I said I'd talk to Sarah," he said. "I'm not talking to anybody else." And to Sarah he said, "Come out here on the balcony, kid."

Mum said, "Sarah! Don't go!"

Donald said, "She won't come to any harm."

Dad said, "Let *me* go out there."

Donald said, "Nobody's coming out on this balcony but Sarah. If anyone else takes a step out here, I jump!"

There were movements behind Sarah. She saw from the corner of her eye that a tall, hefty man had come into the room and was approaching the window. He was in ordinary clothes, but he said quietly to Mum and Dad, "I'm a police officer."

Sarah said, "I *want* to go out there."

Mum said to the policeman, "Don't let her."

But the policeman said, still speaking quietly, "Let her go. It may be the best thing. I'm keeping an eye on her." And as Sarah stepped out through the french window he stood behind her, just inside it.

As she went out, she was conscious of the space around her, the distance to the ground below. It wasn't possible for her to fall over the railing. But she felt instantly dizzy on behalf of Donald. She hadn't much head for heights herself. She couldn't have sat as Donald was sitting now.

"Donald," she said, "get down off the rail. On this side."

Donald stared at her. She stared back at Donald. It was a battle of eyes and wills. Seconds passed like centuries. Slowly, Donald got down from the rail onto the balcony. His eyes slid away from Sarah's and fell on the persuading stick.

"That must be the magic stick I heard about," he said. "You know, kid, I almost believe in it. I'm not going to let it interfere." And with a sudden lunge he grabbed it from Sarah's hand.

She felt the power go at once. She was drained and helpless. For a moment she felt that without the stick she could do nothing. But this was a crisis and she wasn't giving up. She concentrated her mind and clenched her fists. And then she felt strength flowing back into her. She didn't know where it came from. But it wasn't from outside, the way the power of the stick had been. It was inside her, in head and heart, and flowing through her arteries and into every bit of her body, and she was strong to the tips of her fingers and toes.

Donald climbed back on the rail, and sat on it without holding on. In one hand he held the persuading stick, in the other his cigarette, which wasn't much more than a butt. He drew on the cigarette again.

"It's nearly finished, Tiddles," he said. "Give us a goodbye kiss."

Strength surged through Sarah's whole being. She

didn't need the stick at all. She planted her feet apart and looked her brother in the eye.

"Donald Casson," she said, "you are the stupidest person I ever knew. Just you do as you're told. Get down from that rail and put out that cigarette and listen to me!"

It was the tone of command. Donald seemed to wilt before it. He got down from the rail, dropped the cigarette butt, and stamped on it. The persuading stick was inert in his hand, doing nothing.

Sarah said, "Who says you're useless? You'll get a job. You'll get another girlfriend. And if you didn't, you'd still not be useless. *We* want you."

"Can't think why you should want me," Donald muttered.

"Because we love you, you utter thickie!" said Sarah. "Now get in there and don't argue!"

She stepped aside from the french window, making way for him. For a moment it looked as though Donald would resist. Then, head down, he walked past her into the room. As he went, he shoved the persuading stick into her hand.

"Maybe it works after all," he said.

"No, it doesn't," said Sarah. "Not now. Not anymore." She didn't know how she knew that, but she knew it for certain.

As Donald stepped inside the room, the policeman took him gently by the arm.

"That's better, son," he said. "You weren't really going to do it, I know. But you shouldn't scare your folks like that."

Donald said, "How do you know I wouldn't have done it? If it hadn't been for Sarah, maybe I would."

The policeman said, "I think you and me had better have a little talk together, by and by."

Then they both turned in alarm. Mum was bending over Sarah, who'd collapsed in a heap on the carpet.

10

"Shock and exhaustion," said Dr. Lloyd, at the Cassons' house half an hour later. "Not surprising, after an ordeal like that. You have a remarkable daughter, Mrs. Casson. Keep her in bed for a day or two. We'll give her something to help her sleep, and she'll be as right as rain. As for Donald, I think he needs help, and I'll arrange for him to get it. But in my opinion he's a basically sensible young man, and once he's had time to get a grip on himself he'll be all right."

"I just wish he could get a job," said Mum.

"That's something I can't provide him with. They don't supply jobs on prescription."

"He says he's really going to try now. He wasn't trying before."

"Then I dare say he'll succeed. And if he doesn't, it's not a disgrace. He isn't the only one, unfortunately. Now, what's this I hear about a magic wand?"

"It's there on the dressing table," said Mum. "It's just a piece of old tubing. I put it in the trash, but she seems to have got it out again. It was a silly game she was playing. You didn't really believe in that nonsense, did you, Sarah?"

Sarah hesitated. Then she said, "I couldn't do anything with the stick that I wouldn't have been able to do without it."

"Of course you couldn't."

"You're not *afraid* of it in some way, Sarah?" asked Dr. Lloyd.

"No," said Sarah. "Not a bit."

But three days later, when Sarah was up and about, Robin found her in a corner of the garden, behind the compost heap, digging a hole.

"What's that for?" he asked.

"Oh, it's just a hole I'm digging."

"You don't dig holes for fun."

"I can do what I like for fun."

"*I* know what it's for," said Robin. "You're going to bury that stick!"

"What if I am?"

"Nothing. I'm not going to stop you." Then, thoughtfully, "I suppose if you bury it you can dig it up again sometime."

"Oh, no!" said Sarah. "It's never going to come up again."

"Well, then, get on with it," said Robin. "Here, let me have a go!"

Robin loved to be active. In five minutes' time the hole was almost two feet deep. Sarah went and fetched the stick. It was silent and lifeless. Just an old piece of tubing, as Mum had said. She dropped it to the bottom of the hole.

"Rest in peace," said Robin to the stick. He started shoveling earth. Before long the surface was level. Robin dug a little of the soil around the place that had been disturbed, to make it less obvious.

"There you are," he said. "Finished. In a few weeks' time you won't even know where it was. Okay? Now, how about a game of wall tennis?"

11

Beth and Katherine came out of school together. They waited for Sarah, as they always did these days. Then all three of them walked homeward along Barrow Lane.

It was the last day of term, and the last of the school year. Next year they'd be in the top class.

They were carrying their copies of the school magazine, full of stories and poems by pupils.

"Nothing by *me* in it," said Beth.

"Nothing by me, either," said Katherine.

"Nor me," said Sarah.

"There's Emma Radley's story about the magic

wand and the flying horse," said Beth. "Trust *her* to have something in. Three whole pages of it!"

Katherine said, "It's not fair. It was *your* magic wand, Sarah. That's what made Mrs. Freedman tell us to write the story."

Beth said, "That's right. What did you *do* with that stick, Sarah?"

"Oh, it's gone," said Sarah. "It's sort of lost. We won't see it again."

"I'm glad," said Katherine. "I didn't like it. I don't *want* to see it again. There was something about it that I didn't trust."

"It was just an old stick," said Sarah. "It wasn't magic."

"It did things for *you*, though, didn't it?" said Beth.

"It did what I needed," said Sarah. "I don't need it anymore."

They went on their way along Barrow Lane, talking fifteen to the dozen.